PUFFIN BOOKS
RADIO DETECTIVE

Although Laura's father has banned Roundbay
Radio from their flat – and the programme *Cruso's
Island* in particular – she still listens in secretly. She
even enters their poetry competition using a false
name – poetry is one of her favourite hobbies, especially as she knows a real professional poet who
lives next door! All this is fine ... until her poem
wins first prize!

Will Laura manage to keep her identity a secret?
What will happen when Donald, the programme's
young presenter, tries to deliver the prize to
Dominic Frizzel? Will the young detective get to the
bottom of the mystery?

John Escott was born and brought up in Frome,
Somerset, and for the last twenty years has lived in
Bournemouth. He is married with teenage children.

JOHN ESCOTT

RADIO DETECTIVE

Illustrated by Maureen Bradley

PUFFIN BOOKS

PUFFIN BOOKS

Published by the Penguin Group
Penguin Books Ltd, 27 Wrights Lane, London W8 5TZ, England
Penguin Books USA Inc., 375 Hudson Street, New York, New York 10014, USA
Penguin Books Australia Ltd, Ringwood, Victoria, Australia
Penguin Books Canada Ltd, 10 Alcorn Avenue, Toronto, Ontario, Canada M4V 3B2
Penguin Books (NZ) Ltd, 182–190 Wairau Road, Auckland 10, New Zealand

Penguin Books Ltd, Registered Offices: Harmondsworth, Middlesex, England

First published by Hamish Hamilton 1985
Published in Puffin Books 1987
3 5 7 9 10 8 6 4 2

Chapter 1

"Welcome ashore to Cruso's Island ...
Your own very special island ..."

(Opening music fades)

"Hallo, Penny Cruso here. We're together
again for another hour on our desert island."

(Sound of sea and gulls)

"Another hour of letters, competitions and
requests to be read out by our shipwrecked
Crew—Tracy, Donald and Sam. Hi, Crew!"

"HALLO!"

"And hallo, Friday."

(Loud parrot squawk followed by
flapping of wings)

"Right, well we begin with a record
request. Do you have one there Sam?"

Laura's transistor was on the table in the summerhouse. Across the garden—weeds and grass shivering wetly with dew—she could see the window of her parents' bedroom above the kitchen of *The Kingfisher* restaurant.

The curtains were suddenly drawn back and her father appeared in the window, yawning.

Instinctively, Laura reached out and turned down the music on the transistor. Silly really, she thought, because

he couldn't possibly hear it from there.

She frowned, thinking about her father. Why had he suddenly taken such a dislike to Roundbay Radio, the local radio station? And why especially *Cruso's Island*?

"I don't want to hear that silly woman's voice again," Mr Bryant had told Laura, meaning Penny Cruso the presenter of the programme. "In fact, I'm banning the sound of Roundbay Radio from the flat, do you hear?"

Laura had been astonished and was about to put up an argument when she'd caught her mother's look of warning.

"Just put it down to end-of-season tiredness," Mrs Bryant had said to her daughter later. "You know how touchy he gets at the end of summer."

It was true running a restaurant in a

seaside town was extremely hard work, but it wasn't good enough. It still didn't explain why Laura's father had so forcibly taken against the little radio station.

Through the other window of the summerhouse, Laura could see a Collared Dove on the privet hedge that divided Miss Fratt's garden from theirs. It was probably looking at Miss Fratt's aviary, Laura thought, and doesn't know what to make of her tropical birds.

Miss Fratt had bought her bungalow only a year ago but she and Laura had quickly become good friends when they discovered they shared the same hobby—writing poetry.

Miss Fratt was a professional, of course. At least, she was in Laura's view. She'd had two small volumes of poems published and was always willing to advise Laura on her writing.

Unlike Laura's parents, Miss Fratt always managed to find time to talk and, more importantly, to listen. Of course, Laura knew her parents couldn't help being busy. But Miss Fratt, her neat little bungalow crammed with books, her garden full of exotic birds, had become like an adopted 'aunt' to Laura.

Not that Laura told Miss Fratt *everything*.

(Music fades)
"Right, well a little later in the programme we'll be talking to Mr Phillips from the local R S P C A. He'll be answering the questions you've sent in about your pets. But before that, the results of last week's 'write-me-a-poem' competition. Remember? The prize for the winning entry is a book of sea poems, and I asked you to write your own poem about the sea. The best of these will be read out over the next few Saturdays, but this week we'll just hear the winning poem.

"*Donald, would you like to read it out to us?*"

Laura held her breath. This was the moment. Half of her wanted to hear familiar words, the other half didn't.

"'*Sea-washed pebbles beneath my curling toes . . .*'"

Laura's heart stopped.

Or that was how it seemed. There

was a tightening in her chest and her face became prickly hot. On and on went the words from the transistor. Her words. The very words that had once been inside her head, that she'd scribbled out, juggled with, now being heard by hundreds of people.

". . . cries of seagulls, high in the sky, Watch them swoop through the Needle's eye . . ."

Laura silently mouthed the words with him. By the time he came to the last line, she felt as if she might float away into the sky.

"'And the huge emptiness.'"

Laura let out a long breath and tried to stop shaking. She hadn't expected to win. She had thought perhaps hers might have been one of those read out over the coming weeks, but not the outright winner.

A pity about the prize. She would have liked a book of sea poems. But it wouldn't be worth it, not with all the complications with her father when he heard from somebody else—as he surely would—that his daughter had won a Roundbay Radio competition; not when he'd specifically banned the station from the house. No, she'd done the right thing.

"Thank you, Donald. Wasn't that marvellous? Now give us the name of the winner."

"It was sent in by—uh—Dominic Frizzel of Ashtree Road, Penny."

"Well, Dominic, your book of sea poems will be on its way to you today."

Laura wondered what would happen when they discovered there was no such person as Dominic Frizzel living in Ashtree Road, or even in Auksea for that matter.

Chapter 2

Donald stifled a yawn. Tracy Wills noticed and grinned. She was holding the bit of paper with the next request, waiting for Penny to finish telling the *Cruso's Island* listeners about next week's painting competition.

They sat round a circular table, Penny, the three children and Mr Phillips from the R S P C A. In the control room, the other side of a large glass window, sat Greg Wills, Tracy's father. He was a programme presenter and newsreader but also helped out with *Cruso's Island*, putting on the records and fitting in the taped advertisements.

Donald had spent a lot of time with Greg, sitting through the early morning news-and-music programme with him the last couple of Saturdays. It had meant Donald getting up very early but as he planned to be a radio presenter and reporter himself when he grew up, he didn't mind.

After the last record request, Penny brought the programme to a close and they all went out into the main Round-bay Radio office. Penny thanked Mr Phillips for coming whilst Donald fetched a drink from the vending machine.

"I go past Ashtree Road on my way home," Donald told Penny when Mr Phillips had gone.

"Ashtree Road?"

"Where the poetry competition win-ner lives, remember?"

"Ah, yes. You mean you could drop his prize into him?"

"If you like."

"Well, it would save postage," Penny said. "Which would please Mr Munford as he's always going on about keeping postal costs down."

Mr Munford was Programme Controller of Roundbay Radio. He always managed to make Penny nervous which was one of the reasons Donald didn't like him.

Penny put the book into an envelope and handed it to Donald. "Mr Munford isn't too pleased with me at the moment."

"Oh?" Donald said. "Why?"

"I unwittingly upset somebody who was planning to advertise on Roundbay Radio, somebody whom Mr Munford had been trying to persuade. 'And

advertising, Miss Cruso, is the lifeblood
of the station,' he said. 'We must have
more and more of it.' In other words, I
should have been more careful.
Although, thinking about it, there was
nothing I could have done differently."
She shrugged. "Oh well, at least *Cruso's
Island* is going well, even he has to
admit that."

"We're getting lots of entries for the

competitions," Donald agreed. "Anyway, I'll deliver this prize to Dominic Frizzel, whoever he is."

The Roundbay Radio studios were at the end of the cliff road and Donald looked out into the grey mist of Heel Bay as he cycled towards Auksea. The white triangles of three dinghies hovered like ghosts on the flat water. On the beach below, dog-walkers picked their way across the shingle.

Ashtree Road was a turning before the twists and turns of Auksea's narrower streets, a short road with the huge tree from which it took its name at one end. Above this could be seen the square tower of St Mary's Church. The time, Donald saw from the church clock, was eight-twenty. Dominic Frizzel was going to be surprised to receive his prize so quickly. Donald checked the number on the envelope that Penny had addressed. Forty-seven.

It took him just three minutes to discover there was no number forty-seven. It took him another five, making enquiries at several houses, to learn that nobody by the name of Frizzel lived in Ashtree Road.

16

After breakfast, Laura went shopping for her mother. She was on her way back when she bumped into Miss Fratt.

"Hallo, Laura." Miss Fratt was a plump but small woman. She wore brightly coloured clothes—reds and yellows especially—like the plumage of the birds in the aviary in her garden.

"Hallo, Miss Fratt," Laura said.

They walked up the steep hill towards St Mary's Church.

"I'm sure I heard one of your poems on the radio this morning," Miss Fratt said. "But then they said somebody called Dominic Frizzel had written it."

"What? I—I mean, pardon?" Laura almost dropped her mother's shopping.

Miss Fratt smiled. She had noticed how her remark had startled her young

17

friend. In fact, Miss Fratt noticed most things.

"'And the huge emptiness'," Miss Fratt quoted. "I remembered that line because I liked it so much when I first heard it. When you read it to me at the bungalow."

Laura felt very hot. "I didn't know you listened to *Cruso's Island*, Miss Fratt."

"I like Roundbay Radio. It's a very lively little station. Besides, being relatively new to the area, I learn quite a lot." She glanced at Laura. "Sometimes I get surprises."

They had arrived at the entrance to the alleyway through which Miss Fratt would go to reach her bungalow.

"I'd better be getting back," Laura said quickly.

"Won't you come and have some Coke?" Miss Fratt said. "And I bought

some iced buns this morning. They're still warm."

"Well . . ." Laura was fond of iced buns but she had no wish to continue talking about *Cruso's Island.*

Miss Fratt, however, hadn't finished. "Dominic Frizzel is a name I know quite well," she said. "Come on, I'll show you."

There was nothing for it but to go with the old woman.

She knows, Laura thought, following her down the alleyway.

There were lots of books in Miss Fratt's home. The living room had bookshelves around three of its walls. Books, it seemed to Laura, on every subject you could think of, and four shelves of poetry.

Once inside, Miss Fratt went directly to the shelf below the window where

there was a row of dust-jacketed volumes by the same author. She took one out and handed it to Laura.

It was a very old, very faded book. On the cover was the picture of a dead body sprawled on a carpet. Beside the body was a large bird-cage with the door open, the bird gone. *The Cage Bird Deaths* was the title. The author's name was Dominic Frizzel.

"And as that book was published in 1930, I wouldn't think it was the same Dominic Frizzel who wrote the poem *Cruso's Island* broadcast this morning, would you, dear?"

"No," Laura said, her voice faint.

There was a long pause. Then Miss Fratt smiled and said, "Why didn't you use your own name, Laura?"

Laura sighed. "I—I don't know."

"It was a lovely poem. Nothing to be

22

ashamed of, so why borrow a name off one of my books?"

Laura twiddled her fingers, then said, "I suppose I'd better tell you. You don't like mysteries, do you, Miss Fratt?"

Miss Fratt laughed. "Only those I can solve, dear. Here, have a sticky bun whilst I get you a drink, then you can tell me about it."

Chapter 3

"Dominic Frizzel," Mrs Bilsby said. "I seem to know that name."

"You do?" Donald said. "Who is it then? Where does he live?"

"No, I don't know *him*, just that the name seems familiar." Mrs Bilsby heaved the washing machine from under the worktop. "Here, give me a hand, Donald."

On the count of three, Donald and his mother yanked the washing machine into the centre of the kitchen. Mrs Bilsby examined the hose connections at the back.

"Think I'd better get one of these

off," she said. "Might be where the blockage is."

"What's the matter with it?" Donald asked.

"Water's not coming through properly," Mrs Bilsby said. "I asked your father to look at it weeks ago but he still hasn't done it. Mind you, he has had a lot of extra duties at the hospital lately."

Mr Bilsby was a male nurse at Auksea's hospital. Donald went along one evening a week to help out on the hospital radio-bedside service, playing records to the child patients. He had become something of a local "celebrity" since joining *Cruso's Island,* and a lot of the children already knew his voice.

"So where have you heard of Dominic Frizzel?" he asked his mother.

"Mm? Where's the spanner you use on your bike, Donald? I can't shift this nut with my fingers."

"Hang on." Donald went out to the shed and came back with the spanner. "Here you are. Now what about that name?"

"Name?"

Donald sighed. "Dominic Frizzel."

Mrs Bilsby fitted the spanner over the nut and gave it a tug. It didn't budge. "I think it's the name of some writer. Not a modern one though. If it's who I'm thinking of, my mother used to like his books, years ago."

It didn't seem to be much help. Donald couldn't imagine what it could have to do with the poem he'd read out that morning. On the other hand, it wasn't a very common name.

"What sort of books did he write?"

Mrs Bilsby was wrestling with the nut on the hose clip again. "Can't remember. Must have been either love stories or mysteries though because they were the only sorts my mother would read."

Coincidence, Donald thought, it had to be. Then he had an idea and could have kicked himself for not thinking of it earlier.

The phone directory!

There was just one person listed— Frizell (two l's, Donald noted) P. 3, St

Mary's Lane. That was up by the church, a rank of tiny cottages.

"I'm going out," Donald yelled to his mother from the hallway.

"What?" There was a sudden gushing sound and a shriek from the kitchen.

Donald poked his head round the doorway. Mrs Bilsby stood in a pool of water. Donald grinned. "Seems to be coming through properly now."

Mrs Bilsby glared at him.

Mr and Mrs P. Frizell of 3, St Mary's Lane had no children and did not listen to *Cruso's Island*, never mind sending in poems. Whilst they would have liked to help him, they told Donald, they had never heard of Dominic Frizzel.

So that was that. Back to square one, Donald thought.

He was passing the side entrance of St Mary's Church when he saw Mr Kinray coming out. Mr Kinray owned the bookshop down the hill but also looked after the clock in St Mary's tower.

"Hallo, Mr Kinray," Donald said. "Shop closed for dinner?"

The old man nodded and shut the church door behind him. He was a huge man but with very small feet so that each step he took seemed like a balancing act.

It was then Donald remembered that Mr Kinray knew about books and writers.

"Um, have you heard of Dominic Frizzel?" he asked.

Mr Kinray's eyebrows went up. "*I've* heard of him, lad. Though I'm surprised you have."

They walked back down the hill, Donald pushing his bike. He explained about the mysterious competition winner and also what his mother had said.

"She's quite right," Mr Kinray said. "Dominic Frizzel was a writer of detective stories in the 1930s and 1940s. Very popular, too. Nobody reads his stuff these days though and he hasn't written anything for thirty-odd years."

"Oh," Donald said.

"Occasionally I get a second-hand copy of one of his titles, then I phone Cecil Worpington. He collects detective stories, the older the better."

"Mr Worpington of Auksea Pottery?" Donald said, surprised. Mr Worpington was an important man in the town and Auksea Pottery was something of a tourist attraction.

"That's him," Mr Kinray said. They

had reached his shop and he took a key from his pocket. "Well, I hope you find your Dominic Frizzel."

"Me too," Donald said. He was beginning to get the taste for playing detective.

Mr Bryant opened the door of *The Kingfisher*, putting up the 'closed' sign at the same time. He nodded and smiled at the two men who were leaving the restaurant after eating a large and expensive lunch. They were the last two customers to leave.

"Be seeing you again I hope, Mr Worpington," Laura's father said.

One of the two—a tall, dark-suited man with greying hair—patted Mr Bryant on the shoulder. "You certainly will, George. That was a splendid meal. Didn't you think so, Mr O'Connor?"

The other man nodded. "Excellent."

Laura's father reddened with pleasure.

"He's also an expert photographer, Mr O'Connor," Mr Worpington said. "Belongs to the Camera Club of which I'm President."

34

"It's just a hobby," Mr Bryant said.

"But you're good," Mr Worpington told him. "I was surprised you didn't win the Annual competition last month. Came second though, didn't you?"

"That's right," Mr Bryant said.

His voice had a strangled note to it, Laura noticed. She was clearing tables; her mother was wiping glasses behind the tiny bar in the corner.

After the two men had gone, Laura's father stamped across to the bar. "You see? Even Mr Worpington thinks my picture should have won the competition. And if it hadn't been for that wretched Cruso woman!"

Laura looked round quickly.

"It's no good keeping on about it," Mrs Bryant said. "It's over now. There'll be another chance next year. Besides, they have other competitions at the Camera Club, don't they?"

"It's not the same," her husband complained. "It's the Annual that's the most important. And I was certain I'd get it this year. I would have, too, if it hadn't been for that woman. Ted Barker said it was her vote that swung it the other way."

"Ted Barker shouldn't have told you anything of the sort. Isn't it against the rules?"

Mr Bryant muttered something Laura couldn't hear.

"Are you talking about Penny Cruso of Roundbay Radio?" she asked. "Was she one of the judges?"

Her father whirled round, giving a

snort of disgust. "*Guest* judge. And what does she know about photography?"

"I suppose she has an opinion," Mrs Bryant said carefully. "I expect she knows what she likes when she sees it."

"But *technically*," Mr Bryant began.

"That was for the other judges," Mrs Bryant said. "They were the experts. I expect they asked Miss Cruso to judge simply as an ordinary person. Except, of course, she's a personality as well because of Roundbay Radio."

"Yes, well you know what I think of Roundbay Radio. And to think I was planning to take advertising time after that chap Munford down at the Camera Club kept on about it. After the competition, I told him what he could do with his advertising *and* his precious radio station."

So *that* was what it was all about,

Laura thought as she went back up to the flat. *That* was why Roundbay Radio had become a dirty word, had been banned. How unfair! All because of some stupid photography competition.

And what about the competition *she* had won? Laura almost wished now that she had put her real name to the poem. Although her winning something judged by Penny Cruso would only have made her father even more furious.

No, perhaps it was as well she'd hidden behind the pen-name. There was no chance of her identity being discovered providing Miss Fratt said nothing, as she'd promised earlier.

After all, who could possibly find out?

Chapter 4

Donald was trying to remember the
words of the poem. Something in them
had rung a tiny bell in his head, some
thing that made him think he and the
writer were thinking of the same thing.
What was it?

He was cycling along the cliff road
towards the large, white-faced building
of Auksea Pottery. When he reached it,
he parked his bike by the steps outside.

There was a showroom on the
ground floor where you could buy some
of the products, and it was from here
that guided tours of the building were
begun in the summer. Donald had been
round once with a school party.

Today, however, he was more interested in seeing the man whose family had founded the pottery and who was now overall head of the operation— Mr Cecil Worpington.

"Impossible," the receptionist at the showroom desk told Donald. "Mr Worpington only sees people by appointment."

"I'm from Roundbay Radio,"

Donald said, but it made no impression.

"And anyway, he's not back from lunch," the woman said. She wore glasses that curled upwards and gave her a fixed look of astonishment.

Donald glanced at his watch. "It's three o'clock, he takes a long time to eat his dinner."

"Out," the woman said, pointing to the door.

"He comes in on Saturdays, does he?" Donald knew that if he was to become a radio reporter he would have to learn not to give up easily.

"Mr Worpington comes in every day, even Sundays. Now, off you go. The only reason the showrooms are open Saturdays is so that people can buy things, so unless you are about to spend some money..."

Donald retreated to the steps outside.
He was about to mount his bike when
a large, wine-coloured saloon car drew
up. A chauffeur in a peaked grey cap
got out and opened the rear door.

Mr Cecil Worpington got out. Donald had seen the man's picture in the local paper often enough to know who he was.

"Excuse me," Donald began.

"Clear off, son," the chauffeur said, giving Donald a shove.

"Mr Worpington," Donald tried again. Mr Worpington glanced at him but didn't stop. The chauffeur's eye had a threatening gleam. "It's about Dominic Frizzel!"

Mr Worpington paused, turned round and looked at Donald. He smiled. "Now what would somebody of your age know about Dominic Frizzel?" he said. "Perhaps you'd better come up to my office and tell me."

Moments later, they passed an open-mouthed receptionist in the showroom. Donald gave her a wink.

Laura sat on a grassy ledge, halfway down the cliff face. She scribbled swiftly in her notebook, chewing her bottom lip as the pencil flitted across the page. Sometimes the words came fast, like a gush of water, other times they had to be squeezed out of her brain like toothpaste from an empty tube.

The ledge was a private place, out of sight of the main beach. It wasn't a dangerous spot and getting to it was easy enough providing you knew it was here and knew at which point to leave the zig-zag path.

She stopped writing and shut the notebook. Her hand ached but that didn't matter. It had gone well this afternoon. Don't read it now, she told herself, read it tomorrow. It was a trick Miss Fratt had taught her. Tomorrow the poem would read fresh, she would

be able to see where it was right and where it was wrong.

Laura wished she could write poetry as well as Miss Fratt. She took a slim

book from her pocket. *Poems* by Dorothy Fratt, it said on the pale green dust-jacket.

Laura flipped through the pages to find some of her favourites. She had read and re-read them since Miss Fratt had made her a present of the book last Christmas.

She sat reading, the only sound that of the sea splashing around the base of the tall, narrow rock with a hole in the top which stood opposite the ledge. Needle Rock, Laura had named it because it reminded her of a darning needle.

She often wondered if anyone else had noticed the likeness.

Chapter 5

Mr Worpington sat behind a large, leather-topped desk and drummed the tips of his fingers on it.

"Puzzling," he said. "Very puzzling." He had listened to Donald's story. "Do you know what I think? I think somebody used the name instead of their own. Somebody who saw the name somewhere—on a bookshelf in their own home, perhaps, although very few people read Dominic Frizzel today unless they're like me and have a bee in their bonnet about old books."

"Do you really collect detective books?" Donald asked.

"I have over a thousand," Mr Wor-

pington said. "Some were published nearly a hundred years ago."

It seemed an awful lot of books to Donald. "Why do you? Collect them, I mean."

Mr Worpington laughed. "That's a good question. Simply because I like them, I suppose—especially those written before the last war. I like puzzles, mysteries, pitting my wits against the writer, trying to guess the outcome. It's a bit like doing crosswords and jigsaw puzzles. I suppose I have a logical mind, like things neat and orderly. I don't like unanswered questions. Nor do you, Donald, or so it seems. Why else would you be taking so much trouble over finding your mysterious prizewinner?"

Donald nodded. "But why did he use a false name?"

"Ah, well, there you have me."

"You don't think any relatives of Dominic Frizzel live in Auksea, do you?" Donald said.

Mr Worpington shrugged. "Who knows? Dominic Frizzel was something of a mystery himself. Always avoided publicity, never had his picture taken, never gave interviews. Nobody knew who he was except his publishers, and they wouldn't tell you because I tried asking."

"You did?"

"My collection of his books are two titles short—*The Parakeet Murders* and *The Cage Bird Deaths*. I was hoping I might be able to buy copies from the author himself."

"But they wouldn't tell you where he lived?"

"No," Mr Worpington said. "Pity because I'd pay a lot for those two books."

"Birds," Donald said after a moment.

"Pardon?"

"Those two titles. Both to do with birds."

"Oh, yes. Something of an expert on tropical birds, Mr Frizzel. The subject came up somewhere in almost all his books."

Donald stood up from the leather armchair where he'd been sitting. "I'd better be going."

Mr Worpington went down to the showroom with him. "What was the name of that programme of yours?"

"*Cruso's Island*," Donald said.

"Mm, I must listen to it some time. Sounds interesting. A lot of people seem to listen to Roundbay Radio now; I shall have to consider advertising Auksea Pottery on it, perhaps around Christmas. Munford, down at the Camera Club, suggested it some time ago but I told him no. Perhaps I should think again."

"I'm sure it would be a good idea," Donald said, anxious to promote the radio station and do Penny a good turn at the same time.

"Well, I hope you find your competition winner," Mr Worpington said. "I have a feeling it's going to be like looking for a needle in a haystack though. Still, I wish you luck."

He closed the showroom door after Donald who went back to his bike.

Needle!

Donald stopped. Of course, that was it! The line from the poem that he'd been trying to remember; the line that rang a bell.

". . .*watch them swoop through the needle's eye.*"

Gulls swooping through a needle's eye. A rock that looked like a darning needle—especially when you saw it from a particular place. He'd thought so heaps of times, hadn't he?

Donald grabbed his bike.

The wind was getting up. White tips

appeared on the waves around the base of Needle Rock. Laura decided it was time she went home.

They always had a meal before opening the restaurant in the evening and her mother liked her to help prepare it. Mr Bryant only cooked for the restaurant. He had been a chef in one of

Auksea's largest hotels before buying his own business.

It was hard work but things were getting better. They had regulars in and out of season—like Mr Worpington. Mr Bryant considered him one of the most important customers. He always listened attentively to Mr Worpington's opinions and advice.

"He uses *The Kingfisher* often now, and brings important clients with him," Mr Bryant had told his wife only that day.

Laura wished Mr Worpington would tell her father to let them all listen to Roundbay Radio again, she was sure he would take notice. She took a last look at Needle Rock and made her way back towards the zig-zag.

Coming down the zig-zag path on a bike was a boy Laura's own age, or thereabouts. She moved out of his way but he stopped just the same.

"Hallo," he said. "Have you been down to the ledge?"

Laura looked surprised. She didn't know this boy although his voice sounded familiar. "What if I have?"

The boy smiled. He seemed particularly interested in Laura's notebook and Miss Fratt's book of poetry, both of which Laura was carrying. "It's great down there, isn't it?"

Laura nodded and was about to walk on. Then he spoke again and this time what he said made her mouth go dry.

"I like to watch the gulls . . . swooping through the Needle's eye." He paused, smiled, then said, "Do you?"

Laura swallowed slowly. "Wh-what needle?"

Instead of answering, he reached out

58

and took the book of Miss Fratt's poems
from her hand.

"Hey!"

"Do you like poetry?" he said. He
began to quote. "'Cries of seagulls, high
in the sky. Watch them swoop through
the Needle's eye.'"

And then she recognised his voice. It was the same one she'd heard reading her poem that morning.

"Oh," she said.

He grinned and held out a hand. "Dr Frizzel, I presume," he laughed.

Chapter 6

They walked back to the town together, Donald pushing his bike.

"Quite a detective, aren't you?" Laura said when he told her about connecting the description of Needle Rock with the line in the poem.

"Talking about detectives," Donald said. "Where did you get the name, Dominic Frizzel?"

Laura had the feeling he would find out whether she told him or not, he was that sort of boy. "Off the cover of a book on Miss Fratt's shelf," she said.

"Miss Fratt? Now why does that name seem familiar?"

"Because it's on the front of the book you so rudely snatched from me."

Donald looked at the book in his hand. "So it is. Dorothy Fratt. Does she live near you?"

"At the bottom of our garden."

"Like a fairy, you mean."

Laura laughed in spite of herself. "Not really."

"Interesting though, two poets living so close together."

"I'm just a beginner," Laura said.

"Oh, I don't know. Which reminds me, I have your prize at home. Shall I

bring it round to your proper address later?"

"No," Laura said quickly. "It's all right, I'll collect it."

He watched her carefully, then said, "Why didn't you put your own name to the poem? And don't tell me it was because you're shy because I shan't believe you."

"You don't give up, do you?" Laura said. She hesitated, then went on, "Because my father doesn't like Round-bay Radio and has banned me from listening."

"Really? Why?" Donald had never heard of anybody not liking the radio station before.

So Laura explained about the photography competition and Penny Cruso.

"I see," Donald said. "Your father didn't cancel plans for advertising on Roundbay by any chance, I suppose?"

"Yes, he did," Laura said.

"Mm, well it all seems very unfair," Donald said.

"It is. Especially my not being able to listen to *Cruso's Island*."

"Sounds as though you listen just the same."

She grinned. "You bet I do. It's a good little programme."

"Thanks," Donald said. "I'll tell Penny you think so." He looked at the book of poems again. "Unusual name,

Fratt. I seem to be haunted by unusual names today. And she likes detective stories too, does she?"

"I suppose she must," Laura said. "She has a shelf full of Dominic Frizzel books. That's how I came to notice the name."

"She should meet Mr Worpington," Donald said.

"Mr Worpington? Of Auksea Pottery? What's he got to do with it?"

"He collects detective stories," Donald told her. "Hey, that's a thought!"

"What is?"

"I wonder if Miss Fratt has copies of the two books missing from his collection? If she has, he'd pay a pretty penny for them."

Laura shrugged. "She might. Like I said, she's got an awful lot."

Donald looked thoughtful. "Look, do you think you could introduce me to her?"

"I suppose so," Laura said, surprised. "Why?"

Donald leaned against his bike and looked at the book of poems. "She

might just have copies of those two books which she'd be willing to sell."

"She might," Laura agreed. "But why are you so anxious to please Mr Worpington?"

Donald tapped the side of his nose. "Business."

"What sort of business?"

"Advertising," Donald said. "'The lifeblood of the station', as Mr Munford would say. You see, Mr Worpington is thinking of buying advertising time on Roundbay and as somebody who works for the station, I have to help get the business if I can." Besides helping Penny, he thought.

"So you're going to bribe Mr Worpington into taking advertising time for Auksea Pottery in exchange for two detective books," Laura said.

"Of course not," Donald said. "But I

have a feeling if I come up with those missing titles he'll be easier to persuade."

"Let's hope Miss Fratt can help then," Laura said.

There was no reply to Miss Fratt's doorbell.

"She might be in the garden," Laura said. "She has an aviary."

Donald looked at her.

"What's the matter?" Laura said.

"You did say an aviary, didn't you? The sort that has birds in it?"

"What other sorts are there?" Laura wondered if he might be slightly mad. "Come on, I'll lead the way."

Donald followed, strangely silent, deep in thought.

"Miss Fratt?" Laura called.

The old woman was closing the aviary door having come out. "Hallo, Laura. Oh, you've brought a friend."

They stood outside the wire netting. Inside, brightly coloured birds flew like flashes of light.

"This is Donald," Laura said. "He's the one on *Cruso's Island*."

"Ah," Miss Fratt said. "Does that mean—?"

"Yes," Laura said. "He knows I wrote the poem."

"Well, I'm glad," Miss Fratt said. "At least now you'll get the prize, and it's well deserved, isn't it, Donald?"

"Yes," Donald said, then went on, "You write poetry as well, don't you, Miss Fratt?"

"Yes, I do, Donald," Miss Fratt said.

He was looking at the old woman with an odd expression, Laura noticed. In fact his whole manner had become peculiar since she'd mentioned the aviary.

"You remember the name I put to my poem, Miss Fratt?" Laura said.

"Yes, dear. I remember it very well."

"Donald knows somebody who collects books by that author and he was wondering if you had copies of two titles that the man is still looking for. Donald thinks the man would pay a lot of money for them."

"Really?" Miss Fratt said. "I know that Dominic Frizzel books have become—well, collectible over the past few years. What are the names of the two books, can you remember, Donald?"

"*The Parakeet Murders* and *The Cage Bird Deaths*," Donald told her.

She nodded. "Ah, yes. 1929 and 1930. There was just the one edition printed and they're quite difficult to come by. Still, I think I have a spare copy or two."

"A spare copy *or two*?" Donald repeated. "Isn't that unusual, Miss Fratt?

Miss Fratt walked towards the bungalow and they followed. "Unusual?"

"A scarce book," Donald said, "and yet you have more than one spare copy."

Miss Fratt didn't reply but opened the back door of the bungalow.

"What are you doing?" Laura hissed. "Why all these questions?"

"Just an idea," Donald whispered back.

They followed her into a sparkingly tidy kitchen.

"Are you a bit of an expert on tropical birds, Miss Fratt?" Donald asked gently.

"I suppose you could say I was," Miss Fratt told him. "I've always kept them."

They went through to a living room which was neat as a hospital bed. Miss Fratt crossed to the shelves under the window and ran her eye along the titles. She took out two books.

"Here we are." She handed them to Donald.

He frowned. "Shouldn't I tell him to come and see you about them? Fix up a price and everything?"

"I don't want anything for them," Miss Fratt said. "If he really is such a great fan of Dominic Frizzel books then he can have them with my compliments."

Donald nodded, understanding. Laura continued to look puzzled. Why was Miss Fratt giving away something that could be valuable?

"Have you signed them?" Donald asked suddenly.

Miss Fratt's cheeks became flushed. She looked at the flowered carpet. "Signed them?"

"Signed copies are more valuable," Donald said. "Copies signed by the author, that is."

Chapter 7

Laura stared at him. "I don't understand."

Miss Fratt let out a long sigh. "Your friend Donald has guessed something which I've kept a secret for more than fifty years."

"Well, could somebody explain it to me, please?" Laura said. She looked at Donald again. "How can Miss Fratt's signing two Dominic Frizzel books make them more valuable?"

Donald glanced at Miss Fratt before saying, "Because books signed by their authors—especially old, collectible books—are more valuable. And Miss Fratt *is* the author of those two stories,

77

and all the other 'Dominic Frizzel' books as well."

"You mean—?" Laura stared at Miss Fratt. Opened her mouth. Closed it again.

"Miss Fratt is Dominic Frizzel," Donald said.

Laura looked at plump, neat little Miss Fratt, then looked at the dust-jacket of the *The Parakeet Murders* where a huge bird was holding a dagger in its beak, blood dripping from the point, and flying through a stormy sky.

"Some of the best writers of detective fiction were—*are* women," Miss Fratt said, almost apologetically. "Agatha Christie, Dorothy Sayers, P.D. James."

"'Dominic Frizzel'," Donald said. "Why did you stop writing detective books?"

"I finally grew tired of it," Miss Fratt

said. "Besides, I'd become more interested in poetry by then."

"I still don't see how you guessed,"
Laura said to Donald.

"Something Mr Worpington told me
helped," Donald said. "He said Dominic Frizzel was an expert on tropical
birds, that his books always contained
something about them."

"So that's why you looked peculiar
when I said Miss Fratt had an aviary."

"Right," Donald said. "And who but
the author is likely to have more than
one copy of a scarce book—and be
prepared to give it away to an old fan?"

Miss Fratt smiled. "You're quite a
detective yourself, Donald."

"Then there were the two names,"
Donald went on. "Dominic Frizzel.
Dorothy Fratt. Had you noticed? Both
the same initials—D.F."

"So they are," Laura said. "I hadn't noticed."

"The other thing Mr Worpington told me was that Dominic Frizzel was always a mystery. Never had his photo taken, never gave interviews, always avoided publicity—as though he wanted to keep his whole identity a secret." He looked at Laura. "What did you do when you chose a pen-name for yourself? You chose a *man's name*."

"That's right," Laura said. "I thought it would throw people off the track even more."

"You were right," Donald said. He turned to Miss Fratt. "And so were you."

"Until today," Miss Fratt said. "But then, I hadn't made allowances for somebody else choosing the same pen-name, nor for a very wideawake young man from *Cruso's Island.*" She sat down in an armchair and signalled for them to do the same. "The point is, having found all this out, can you both *keep* a secret? After all this time I've no wish

for it to be known I'm Dominic Frizzel. I'm far too old for all the fuss that would result from it."

"We won't say a word," Laura promised. "At least, I won't."

"Nor me," Donald said. "Pity though, because you'd make a marvellous guest for *Cruso's Island*. We've never had a detective story writer on the programme." He sighed. "But I won't say anything."

"You're right about one thing, Donald," Miss Fratt said. "If I give those books to your gentleman it's bound to arouse his suspicions just as it did yours. Perhaps I'd better let him buy them, and you can act as my agent."

"Right," Donald said. He smiled, and Laura knew he was thinking of the Roundbay Radio advertising again.

"Now you can tell me about the rest of your investigating," Miss Fratt said. "The bit that led you to discover Laura was your competition winner."

"Another piece of amazing deduction by our famous Roundbay Radio Detective," Laura said heavily.

Chapter 8

(Fade in closing music . . .)

"Well, that's it for another Saturday. I'd like to thank the Crew, Donald, Tracy and Sam. And special thanks to our guest this morning, Mr Cecil Worpington, who has been telling us all about Auksea Pottery and about his hobby of collecting detective stories. Thanks again, Mr Worpington."

"My pleasure, Penny."

"So, say goodbye, Crew."

"'BYE"

"And goodbye from me, Penny Cruso, until next Saturday. 'Bye!"

The programme over, Penny and Donald watched Mr Worpington and Mr Munford chatting outside the Programme Controller's office.

"You know Auksea Pottery is going to advertise on Roundbay, I suppose," Penny said to Donald. "Thanks to you."

"Uh—yes, I did."

"And *The Kingfisher* restaurant, would you believe? Apparently that was Mr Worpington's suggestion and the restaurant owner takes a lot of notice of what our programme guest tells him."

"Great," Donald said. At least Laura wouldn't have to listen to *Cruso's Island* in secret any more.

The chairman of Auksea Pottery had been both astounded and delighted when Donald had turned up with both his missing Dominic Frizzel books.

"Where on earth did you find them?" Mr Worpington had asked.

"Somebody I met through being on *Cruso's Island*," Donald told him, quite truthfully.

It had been more than enough to convince the man what a "splendid little radio station" Roundbay was, so Donald had followed this up by asking Mr Worpington to come on *Cruso's Island* as a guest.

"Perhaps I will," Mr Worpington had said. "That programme of yours seems to be full of surprises."

Which, as Donald had already proved, was perfectly true.